GEORGIE

GEORGIE

By ROBERT BRIGHT

SCHOLASTIC INC.
New York Toronto London Auckland Sydney

ISBN 0-590-42126-3

Copyright 1944 by Doubleday & Co., Inc. This edition is published by Scholastic Book Services, a division of Scholastic Magazines, Inc., by arrangement with Doubleday & Co., Inc.

6 5 4 3   8 9/8 0 1 2 3/9

For
Robin and Beatrice

In a little village in New England there was a little house which belonged to Mr. and Mrs. Whittaker.

Up in the little attic of this little house there lived a little ghost. His name was Georgie.

Every night, at the same time, he gave the loose board on
the stairs a little creak,

and the parlor door a little squeak.

And then Mr. and Mrs. Whittaker knew it was time to go to bed.

And Herman, the cat, he knew it was time to prowl.

And as for Miss Oliver, the owl, she knew it was time to wake up and say "Whoo-oo-oo!"

And so it went, with
everything as it should be,
until Mr. Whittaker took
it into his head to hammer a
nail into the loose board
on the stairs,

and to oil the hinges of the parlor door.

So . . . the stairs wouldn't creak any more

and the door wouldn't squeak any more.

And Mr. and Mrs. Whittaker didn't know when it was time to go to bed any more.

And Herman, he didn't know when it was time to begin
to prowl any more.

And as for Miss Oliver, she
didn't know when to wake up
any more, and went on sleeping.

And Georgie sat up in the attic and moped.

That was a fine how-do-you-do!

Pretty soon, though, Georgie decided to find some other house to haunt.

He ran to this house,

and then to that house,

but each house already had a ghost.

The only house in the whole village which didn't have a ghost was Mr. Gloams' place.

But that was so awfully gloomy!

The big door *groaned* so!

And the big stairway *moaned* so!

And besides, Mr. Gloams himself was such a crotchety old man, he came near frightening Georgie half to death.

So Georgie ran away to a cow barn where there lived a
harmless cow.

But the cow paid no attention to Georgie.
She just chewed her cud all the time, and it wasn't much fun.

Meanwhile a lot of time went by and it rained a good deal.

And during the winter it snowed to beat the band.

And out at the cow barn Georgie was terribly cold and uncomfortable.

BUT...

what with the dampness from the rain and the coldness from the snow, something happened to that board on the Whittaker stairs and to the hinges on the Whittaker parlor door.

It was Herman who discovered it and told Miss Oliver.

She woke up with a start.

Miss Oliver flew right over to the cow barn to tell Georgie that the board on the stairs was loose again, and that the hinges on the parlor door were rusty again.

What glad tidings for Georgie!
He ran right home, lickety-split.

WELCOME

And so, at the same old time, the stairs creaked again.

And the parlor door squeaked again.

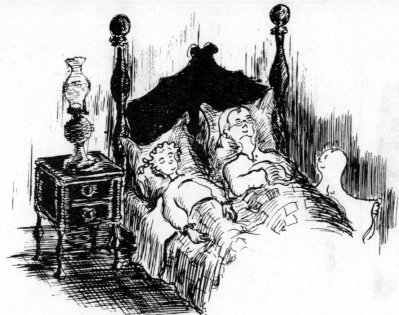

And Mr. and Mrs. Whittaker
knew it was time to go to
sleep again.

And Herman, he knew when
to begin to prowl again.

And as for Miss Oliver, she knew when it was time to
wake up again and say "Whoo-oo-oo!"

THANK GOODNESS!